The Fallen Fairy of Baile

ISBN: 978-0-9987732-0-9

Cover illustration by A. Temborskaya

First Edition

The Fallen Fairy of Baile

Created by E.S. Fortune

Written by Emily Regan

Illustrated by A. Temborskaya

Once upon a time, deep in the woods,

there was fairy kingdom called Baile, ruled by Queen Máthair

and her three daughters. The queen loved all of her children but

she loved her youngest, Eva Aerona, the best of all.

Eva Aerona was good and kind and beautiful,

but she was not admired by everyone.

Her sisters, Invidia, the eldest, and Aemilia grew
jealous and spiteful until it gnawed away at their hearts,
destroying their love for their sister,
and they decided to punish her.

The fairies had free reign of the forest but
in the dark part of the woods was a place called Olc Críoch
Queen Máthair had decreed that no fairy should
ever enter that place, lest they be banished from Baile.
But one day, Invidia and Aemilia approached their
youngest sister with a dark plan betwixt them.
They whispered to Eva Aerona they were going to
Olc Críoch and they asked her to come with them

Eva Aerona gasped and protested
that it was forbidden,
afraid of even the name
of the dark place.
But her sisters insisted that
because Eva Aerona was
so beloved by the queen,
she would not be punished.
They told Eva Aerona of the
ancient secrets in Olc Crioch
that she, and only she, could learn
as the youngest
princess. The elder sisters promised
Eva Aerona
that by learning about this magic
in Olc Crioch,
she could make the
kingdom stronger
and please the queen.

Eva Aerona was unsure, but she agreed
because she loved her sisters and she loved Queen Máthair.
Never before had a fairy ever returned from Olc Críoch
and, although she would not admit it aloud, Eva Aerona
was curious about the dark place

On the next full moon, the three sisters
set out for Olc Crioch together in the starlit woods.
As they journeyed, Eva Aerona felt happy to be
with her sisters, unaware of the anger in their hearts.
Along the way, they were stopped by
an old druid who halted their progress.

Aemilia commanded the man to move, but he did not.
The old druid told them he knew where the three
sisters journeyed, but warned them to turn back.
Each of the sisters felt afraid,
in their own way, but
it was Invidia who spoke first,
commanding her
younger sisters to not listen
to such a fool.
Invidia urged her
sisters forward and
they obeyed.

Only Eva Aerona looked
back and heard the old druid's
parting words, warning of a fool heeding
nothing but their own desires. Eva
Aerona wanted to ask what that
meant, but she was
pulled deeper into the
woods by her
sisters and
so the old druid faded
into the darkness
behind them.

When the full moon was highest in the sky, the three sisters
reached the edge of Olc Críoch.
The elder sisters, careful
not to cross the boundary, urged
Eva Aerona forward.
Eva Aerona begged them to come
with her, but her sisters
shook their heads.
They told her that because
she was the beloved, only she
could do what no other fairy
could. And so Eva Aerona
stepped into the
dark place alone, at the
encouragement of
her sisters.

At first, nothing happened. It could have been any other part of the woods. Eva Aerona paused and looked back to her sisters, who watched expectantly.

She turned forward again and tried to take another
step but found she could not. She looked down and found her
feet bound to the e rth by dark, stinging nettles
that bit her skin.

Eva Aerona cried out to her sisters for help
but they did nothing, watching silently from the safety
of the boundary. Eva Aerona clawed at the nettles to
free herself until she cried and her hands bled but to no avail.

Suddenly, the three sisters
heard the flap
of large wings
in the night air.

A crow landed on the earth, not far from
where Eva Aerona was caught. Invidia and Aemilia
clung to one another,
frightened of the bird,
and began to back away from
the dark place.

The crow towered over Eva Aerona, who wept and pleaded and called for her sisters. The crow said nothing, but regarded her silently, without pity.

Then it snatched Eva Aerona from the nettles in its sharp beak. Eva Aerona screamed as the crow broke and crunched her body and her sisters fled in fear, disappearing into the woods.

The crow was about to deliver the final blow
to Eva Aerona when it suddenly stopped.
It cocked its head listening to something deep
within the dark place.

Eva Aerona slid
from its
beak, falling to
the ground,
and although her body was
broken, she pulled herself
over the unforgiving ground
until she reached the
edge of Olc Crioch. She clung to
the dewy grass,
using the last of her strength,
until she had escaped.

Eva Aerona looked back to the crow,
who had watched her struggle but no longer looked
hungry or pursuant of the crumbling fairy.

Eva Aerona rolled on to her back and stared up at the sky, crying to the stars as her tears mixed with the dew on the forest floor.

The next morning, as the sun rose in the east,
the early light stirred the last of Eva Aerona's
magical strength for her return to Baile.

The journey was longer
than it had been the night before,
and far more painful, but
still she pushed on, determined
to find her home.
She traveled all day
and as dusk was settling
in the woods,
Eva Aerona
finally reached Baile.

Queen Máthair, flanked by her eldest daughters,
waited for her with the whole of the kingdom
behind them. With tears in her voice, Queen Máthair
banished Eva Aerona from Baile,
for there were no exceptions to the official decree.

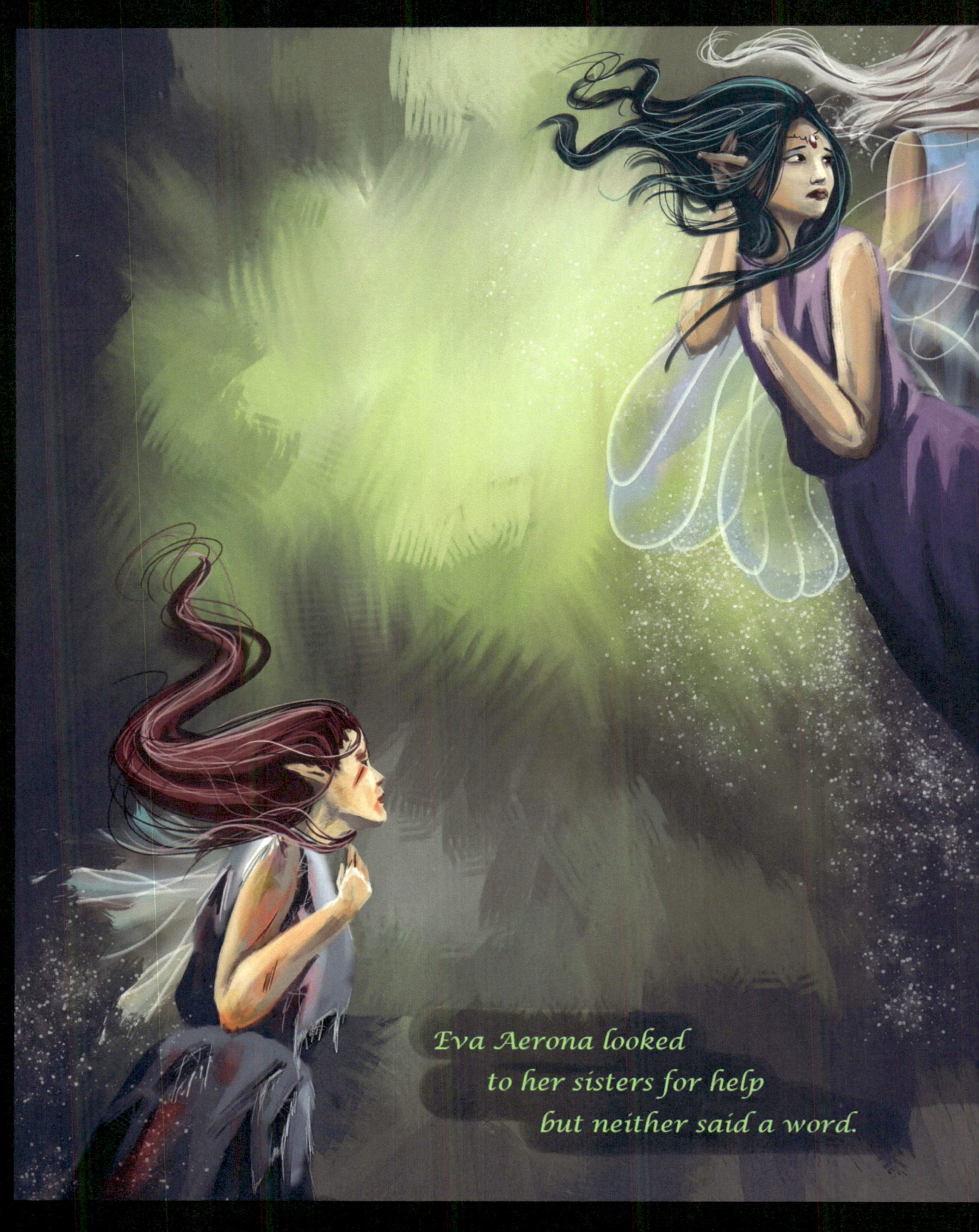

Eva Aerona looked
to her sisters for help
but neither said a word.

And so, Eva Aerona turned
and retreated back into the woods,
forever leaving behind the only home
she had ever known.

E.S. Fortune is the evil genius behind 1602 Enterprises. When he's not running an empire or concocting weird and wonderful stories, he enjoys spending time with his three kids in his home state of Texas.

Emily Regan received her M.A. in creative writing from Northern Arizona University and is the author of several books, including the recent *What's an Adult? No One Knows Anything and We're All Going to Die*. She currently resides in northern Arizona with her husband, son, and two dogs who sit patiently at her feet while she writes (the dogs, not the husband and son).

A. Temborskaya is a digital artist from Ukraine. She is a self-taught artist who enjoys spending most of her free time drawing and improving her skills. She enjoys working on a diverse range of projects and is always trying to create the best solutions to create amazing results.

www.ingramcontent.com/pod-product-compliance
Lightning Source LLC
Chambersburg PA
CBHW041543240626
47164CB00002B/108